Pirate things to make and do

Rebecca Gilpin

Designed and illustrated by Erica Harrison

Additional illustrations by Katie Lovell, Jan McCafferty and Rachel Wells
Steps illustrated by Molly Sage

Edited by Fiona Watt

Photographs by Howard Allman and Edward Allwright

TEACHING RESOURCES COLLECTION
UNIVERSITY OF GLOUCESTERSHIRE
FCH Learning Centre, Cheltenham, GL50 4AZ
Tel: (01242) 532913

Contents

Pirate hats

Rounded hat

1. Fold a large piece of black paper in half. With the fold at the top, lay a small plate on the paper, touching the bottom edge.

2. Draw around the plate. Then, draw curved lines going from either side of the circle to the edge of the paper, like this.

3. Holding the layers together, cut along the curved lines and around the top of the circle. Then, erase the remaining line.

4. Draw a skull and two bones on white paper. Cut them out and glue them onto one of the hat shapes. Then, glue the hat, like this.

Pointed hat

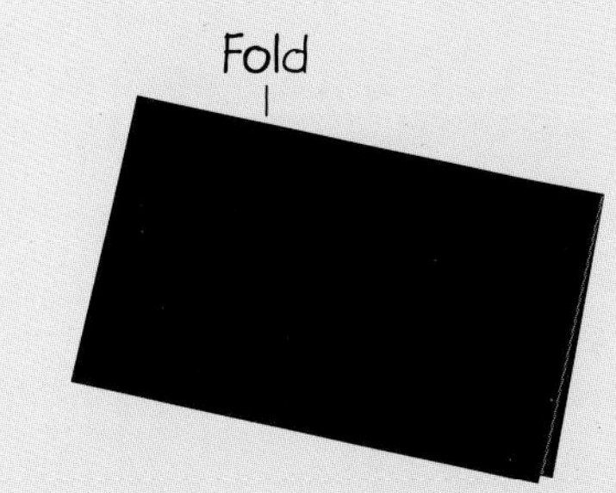

1. Fold a large piece of black paper in half. Crease the fold well. Then, turn the paper, so that the fold is at the top.

2. Bend the paper over so that the short edges meet. Gently squeeze the middle, like this, to make a mark. Then, open it out again.

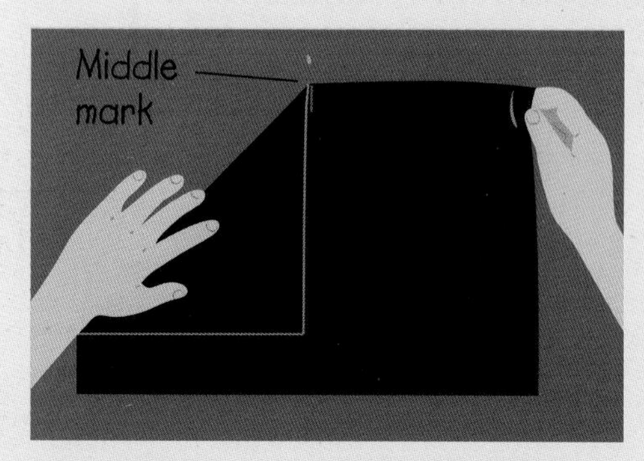

3. Fold the top left-hand corner down into the middle, then crease it flat. Then, fold down the top right-hand corner, too.

4. Fold up the top layer of paper at the bottom of the hat. Then, turn the hat over and fold the other layer in the same way.

5. Cut a circle from white paper. Draw a skull with two crossed bones below it on the paper. Then, glue the circle onto the hat.

If you're dressing up as a pirate, wear a striped T-shirt with your hat.

Find out how to make an eye patch to wear with your hat on page 11.

Pirate ship painting

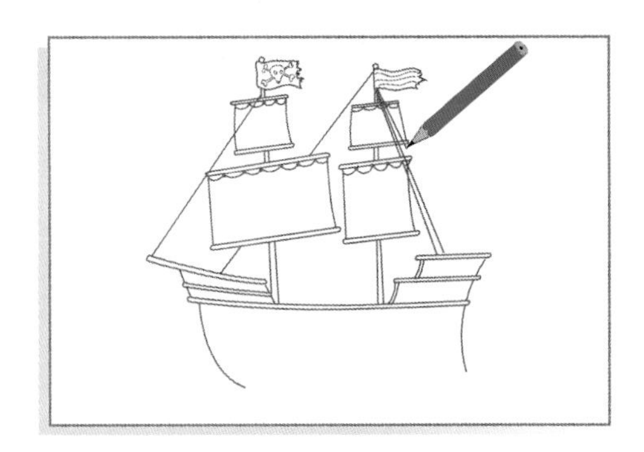

1. Draw a pirate ship on a large piece of white paper. Add two masts, sails and flags. Then, draw some ropes and netting.

2. Draw waves around the ship. Then, draw lots of circles for the pirates' heads. Add a body below each head.

3. Draw headscarves, hats and hair on the pirates' heads. Add their faces and beards, then draw their clothes and swords.

4. Draw a line of round portholes and some arched windows on the ship. Add an anchor, then draw lots of lines for wooden planks.

Try drawing a pirate hanging off the ship or climbing on the netting.

5. Using runny paint, paint the ship and the sea. Fill in the pirates' faces, hands and feet, then paint their clothes and swords.

6. Leave the paint to dry completely. Then, using a thin black felt-tip pen, draw over all the pencil lines you have drawn.

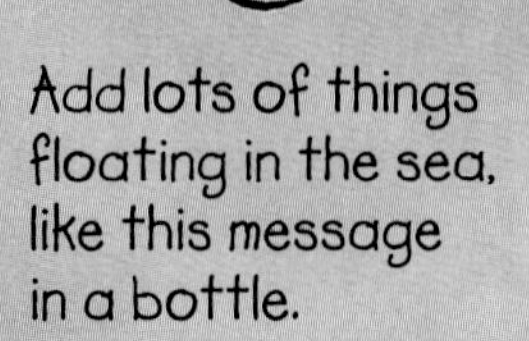

Add lots of things floating in the sea, like this message in a bottle.

You could draw a parrot sitting on a pirate's shoulder.

Money bags

Silver coins

The lid of a spice jar is ideal.

1. To make a silver coin, lay the lid of a small jar on a piece of thin cardboard and draw around it twice. Then, cut out the circles.

Glue the circles onto the non-shiny side.

2. Glue the circles onto a piece of kitchen foil. Then, cut around them, leaving a border. Bend the foil over the edges of the circles.

Be careful not to tear the foil.

3. Using a blunt pencil, draw dots around the edge of each circle. Draw a picture in the middle. Then, glue the circles together.

You could make gold coins from a chocolate wrapper.

To make different-sized coins, use more than one size of lid.

Drawstring money bags

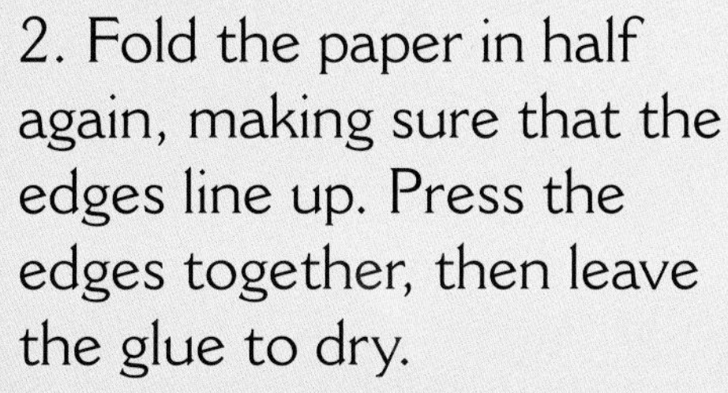

1. Fold a long piece of crêpe paper in half, then open it out. Spread glue along the edges of one half, like this.

2. Fold the paper in half again, making sure that the edges line up. Press the edges together, then leave the glue to dry.

The hole goes through all the layers.

3. Fold the bag in half lengthways, twice. Using one side of a hole puncher, make a hole a third of the way down the bag.

4. Draw a skull and four bones on a piece of paper and cut them out. Draw a face on the skull, then glue the shapes onto the bag.

5. Thread a long piece of ribbon in and out of the holes around the bag. Fill the bag with coins, then tie the ends of the ribbon.

Ancient treasure map

1. To make a piece of white paper look old, rip little strips from around its edges. Tightly crumple the paper, then open it out.

The tea will make the paper turn brown.

2. Pour some cold, strong tea into a dish. Then, lay the paper in the tea and push it down, so that the tea completely covers it.

3. Leave the paper to soak for about an hour. Then, lift it out and lay it on a piece of plastic foodwrap until it is dry.

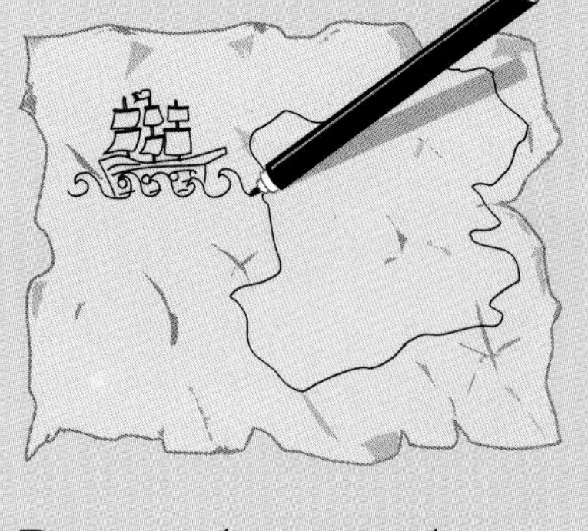

4. Draw a big wiggly shape, for a treasure island. Then, draw a pirate ship and some waves near the top of the map.

5. Draw a flag and write 'TREASURE MAP' next to it. Add a compass in one corner, then draw some rocks around the island.

You could draw a map with lots of small islands instead of one big one.

6. Add waves and sharks' fins, for a shark-infested sea. Then, on the island, draw lots of dangers and write names next to them.

7. Fill in your picture with pencils. Then, mark where the treasure is hidden with a red 'X' and draw a dotted line from the ship to the X.

Pirate paraphernalia

Telescope

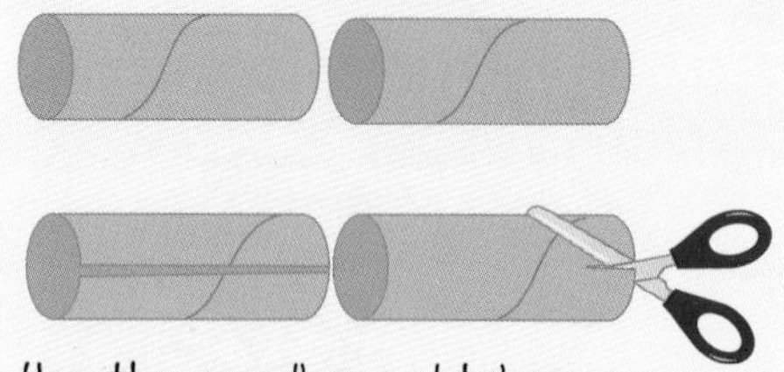

Use the cardboard tubes from inside rolls of paper towels.

1. Very carefully, cut two cardboard tubes in half with a bread knife. Then, cut two pieces from end to end with scissors.

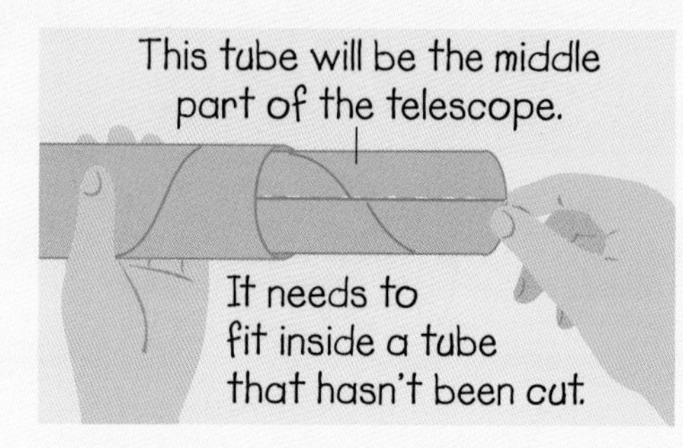

2. Spread glue next to the cut edge of one of the tubes. Overlap the two sides of the cut and hold them together tightly.

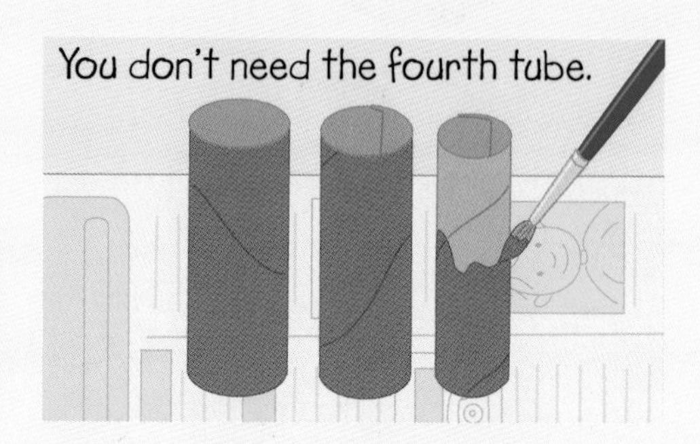

3. Glue the edge of the other cut tube. Overlap its edges, until it fits inside the middle part. When the glue is dry, paint the tubes.

4. Cut a strip of cardboard. Glue it around the widest tube, then glue a thin strip on top. Then, do the same with the narrow tube.

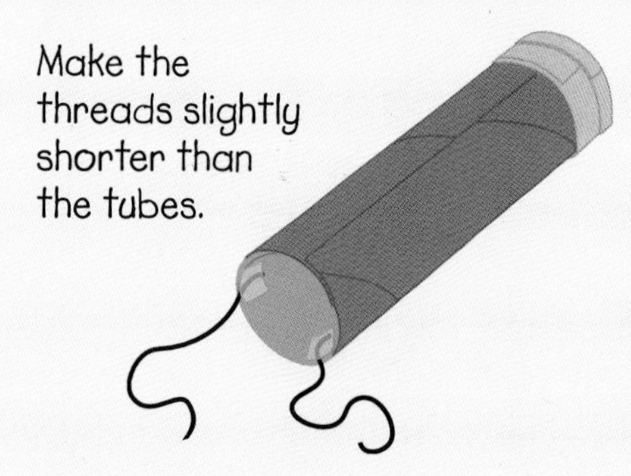

5. To hold the three parts of the telescope together, cut four pieces of thread. Tape two of them inside the narrow tube, like this.

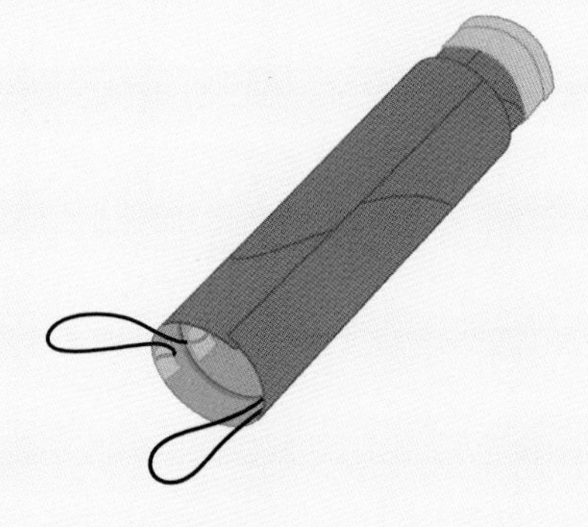

6. Slide the narrow tube inside the middle one. Tape the loose ends of the threads inside the end of the middle tube.

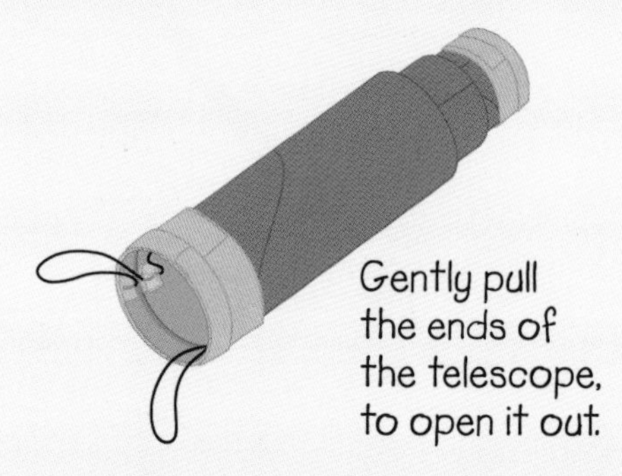

7. Tape the other two pieces of thread inside the middle tube. Slide it inside the widest one, then tape the ends of the threads.

This telescope was decorated with stickers from the sticker pages.

Shiny earring

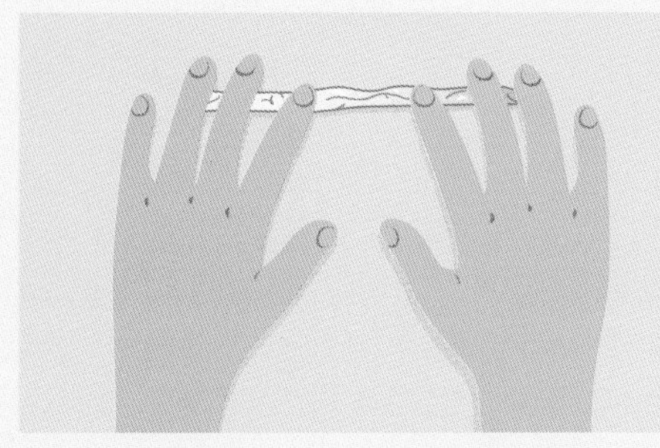

1. Cut a piece of foil that is about the size of a postcard. Squeeze it in your fingers, then roll it on a flat surface, to make a thin stick.

2. Bend the stick into a circle, then twist the ends together. Wrap a small piece of foil around the part where they join.

3. Lay the earring over a thin rubber band that will go around your ear. Then, push one end of the rubber band through the other.

Eye patch

Make the patch big enough to cover one of your eyes.

1. Draw an eye patch, then cut it out. Make a cut into it, then spread glue next to the cut. Overlap the edges and hold them together.

Tie the thread around your head.

2. Cut a piece of thread that will go around your head, plus some extra for tying it on. Tape it to the back of the eye patch.

You could glue cardboard shapes onto your telescope.

Find out how to make a ship's rat on page 17.

Pirate door sign

Hang the door sign from the handle of your bedroom door.

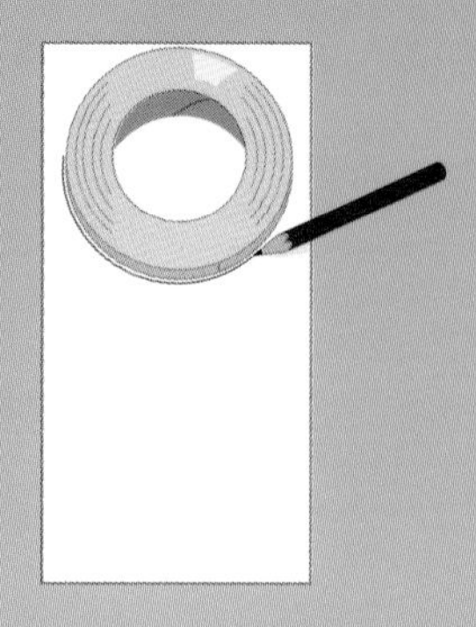

1. Lay a roll of sticky tape near the top of a long piece of thick paper. Then, draw around the tape with a pencil.

Use the lid of a spice jar.

2. Draw two lines from the circle to the bottom of the paper. Lay the lid of a small jar in the middle of the circle and draw around it.

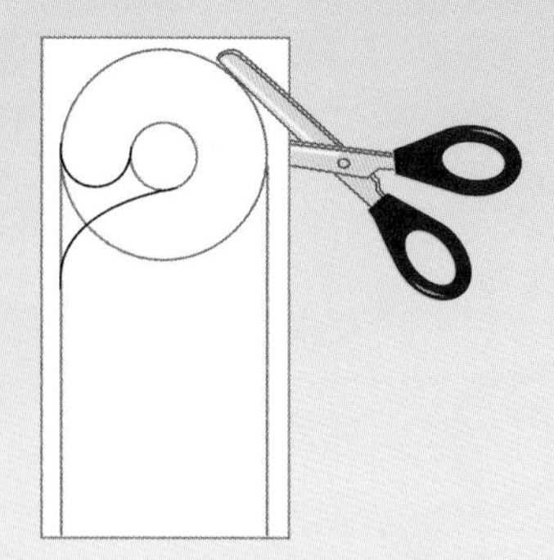

3. Draw two curving lines from the small circle, like this. Then, cut out the door sign shape, along the pencil lines.

To make this door sign, draw a tree in step 4, then add a pirate and an island.

4. Using a pencil, draw a pirate's head halfway down the main part of the sign. Add a headscarf, hair and ears, then draw his face.

5. Draw his body, arms and sword, then draw over all the lines with a black felt-tip pen. Fill in the picture with other pens.

6. Draw stripes across the sign and fill them in with a red pen. Then, write your name or a message on the pirate's sword.

Crew's crazy feast

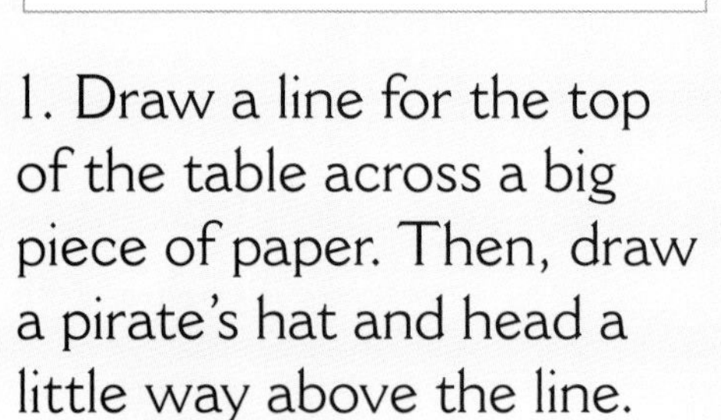

1. Draw a line for the top of the table across a big piece of paper. Then, draw a pirate's hat and head a little way above the line.

2. Draw the pirate's body, with an arm across it. Draw his face, then draw wavy lines on his shirt and stitching on his jacket.

3. Draw more pirates along the table. Outline them all with a black felt-tip pen. Then, fill them in with other bright pens.

4. Cut a long piece of patterned paper for the tablecloth. Glue it onto the picture, lining it up with the pencil line.

5. Cut lots of pictures of food from old magazines. Then, glue the pictures onto the table for the feast, overlapping most of them.

6. To make a pirate hold something, cut out its middle section. Glue one part above and one part below his hand.

Pirate flags

Cut shapes from foil, like the sword below, or press on stickers from this book.

1. For the flags, fold several narrow rectangles of paper in half, with their short ends together. Crease each fold well.

You could draw stripes on some of the flags with a felt-tip pen.

2. With the fold at the top, draw an upside-down 'V' at the bottom of each flag. Then, cut along the lines, keeping the layers together.

3. Draw skulls and bones, anchors, flags and palm trees on pieces of paper. Cut out the shapes and glue them onto the flags.

The glue stops the flags from sliding along the thread.

4. Open out the flags and spread glue along the folds. Fold the flags over a long piece of thread and press the glued parts together.

100
50

50
100

Ship's rats

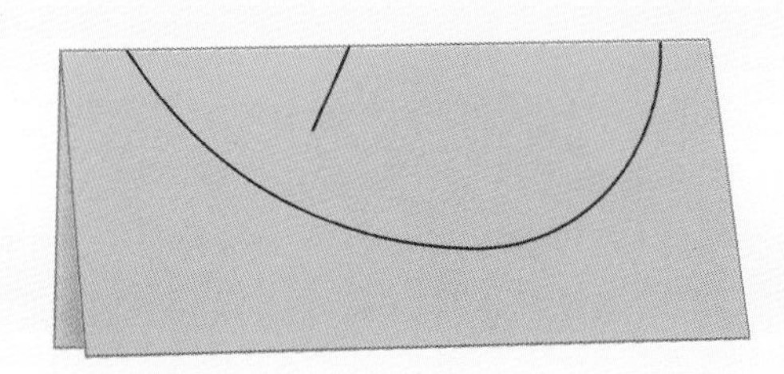

1. For a rat's body, fold a piece of thick paper in half. Draw a curve against the fold and a short line down from the fold, like this.

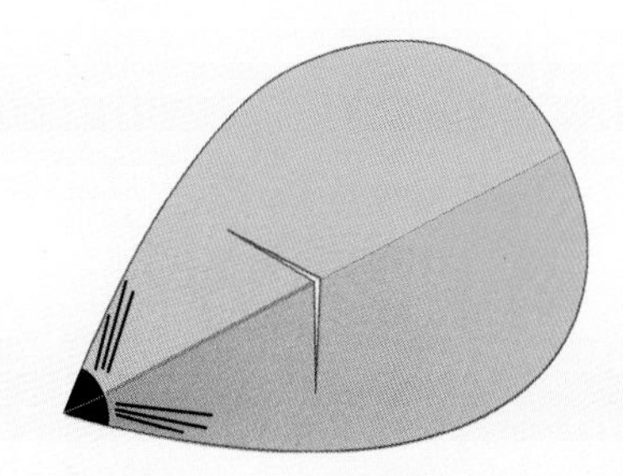

2. Keeping the paper folded, cut along the curve and the short line. Then, flatten the body and draw a nose and whiskers.

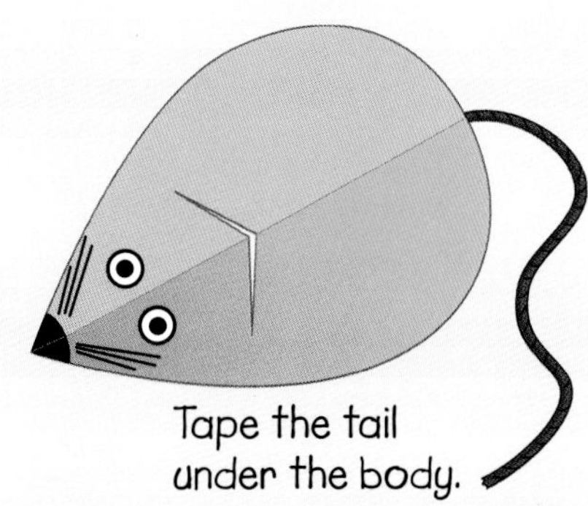

3. Draw two eyes on white paper, then cut them out. Glue them onto the body. Then, for a tail, cut a piece of thread and tape it on.

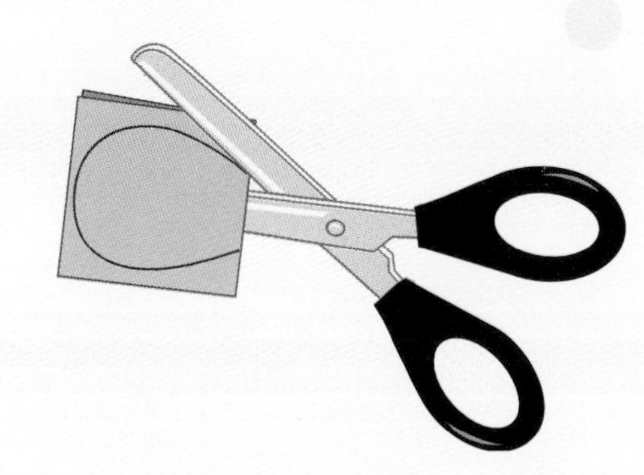

4. Fold another piece of paper in half, for the rat's ears. Draw an ear against the fold, then cut along the line. Open out the ears.

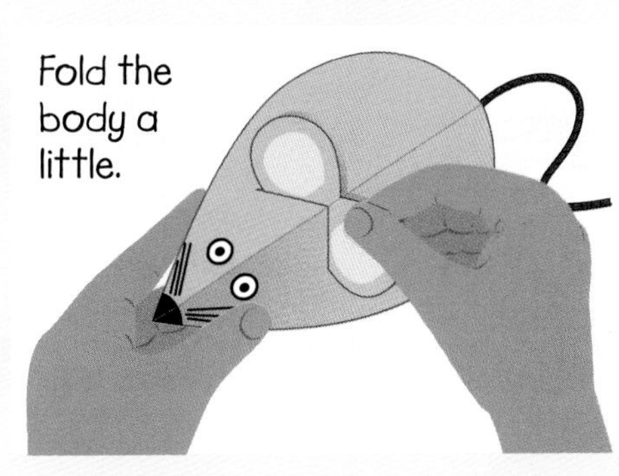

5. Cut two shapes from pink paper and glue them onto the ears. Then, slot the ears into the cut at the top of the body.

Man overboard

The wax resists the paint.

The salt makes a watery effect.

1. Using a white or pale blue wax crayon, draw lots of curling waves across the bottom of a long sheet of white paper.

2. Mix some blue paint with water, to make it watery. Paint over the top line of the waves, then fill in the area below the line.

3. Brush more paint over the wet paint. Then, while it is still wet, sprinkle salt over it. Leave the paint to dry completely.

You could add a shark's fin or a floating barrel to another row of waves.

4. When the paint is dry, brush off any excess salt. Then, draw a pirate ship, with masts and sails, near one end of the painting.

5. At the other end of the paper from the ship, draw a circle for a pirate's head. Add a headscarf and a face, then draw the arms.

6. Paint the ship and the pirate, then leave them to dry. When they are dry, go over the lines with a thin black felt-tip pen.

This big picture was made by cutting out two rows of waves and gluing them together.

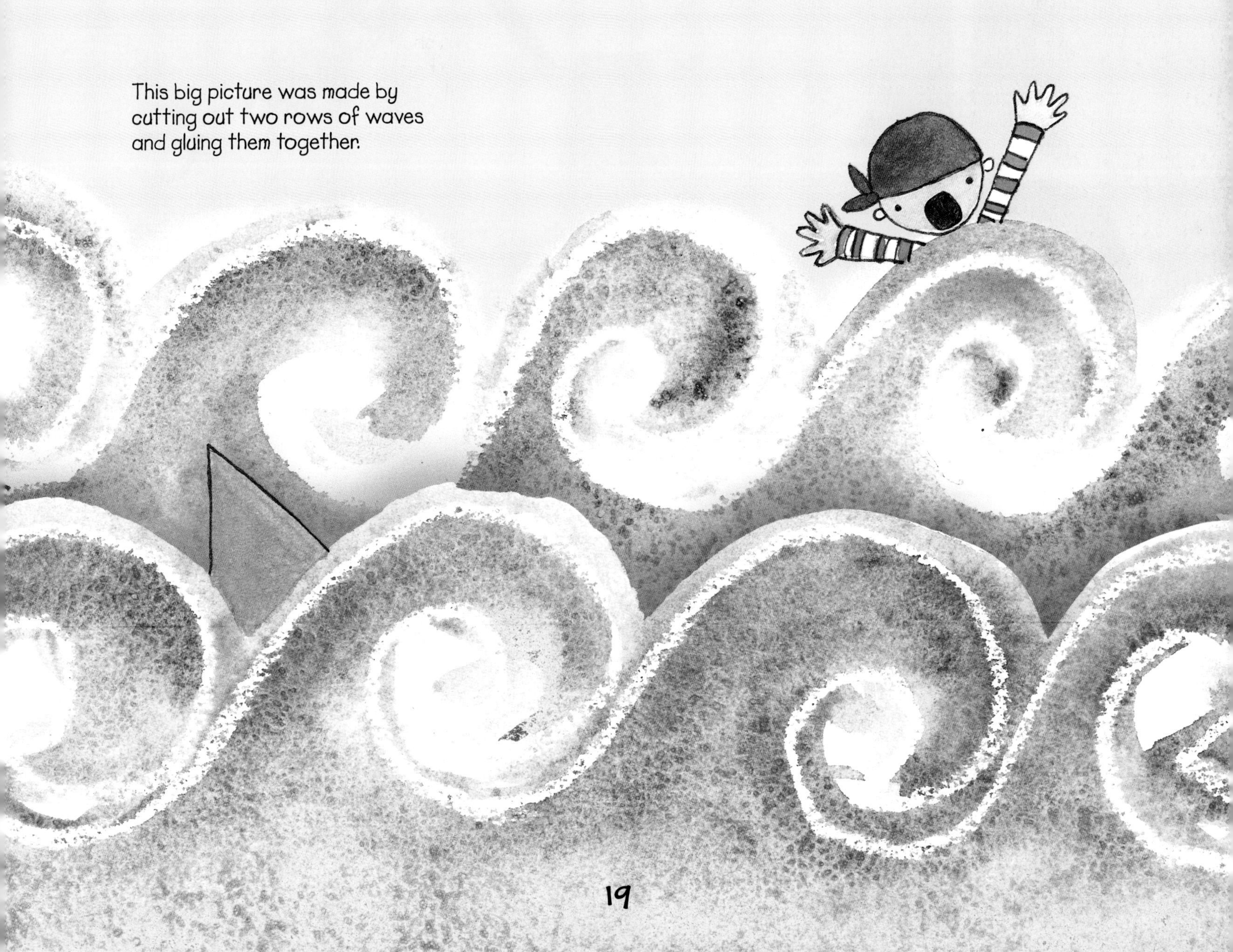

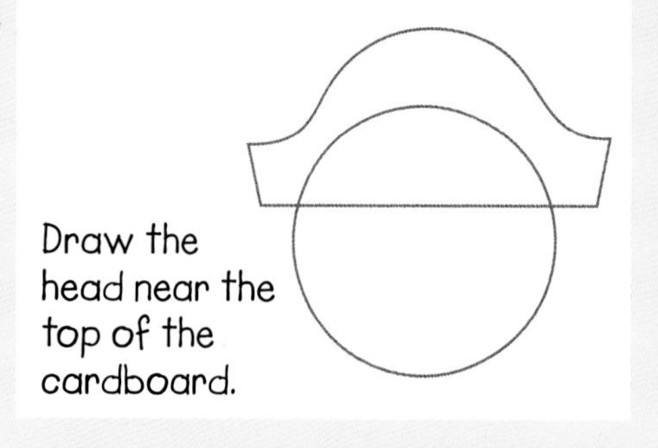

1. For the head, draw a circle on a piece of thin cardboard. Draw a line across the circle, then draw a hat above the line.

2. Add a scarf below the hat, then draw ears and a face. Draw a body and two arms. Then, add two lines down the body.

3. Draw a pair of shorts on black paper and cut them out. Lay them below the body and draw around them. Then, lift them off.

4. Draw a circle on each leg. Use felt-tip pens to draw over all the lines and fill in the clothes. Then, cut around the pirate.

5. Cut up into the circles, then cut around them. Spread glue along the top of the shorts and press them onto his legs.

6. For the pirate's boots, draw a boot on thick paper, making the leg part as wide as two fingers, like this. Then, cut it out.

Push your fingers through the holes, then push on the boots and wiggle your fingers.

The tab is used when you glue the boots together.

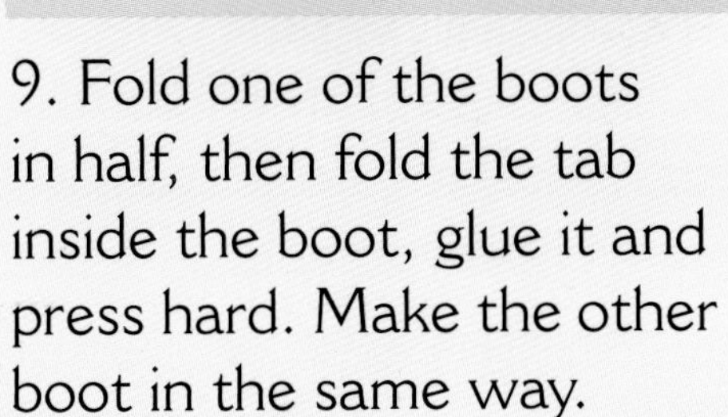

7. Fold a piece of paper in half and lay the boot on it. Draw around the boot, then turn it over and draw around it again, like this.

8. Draw a tab on the side of one of the boot outlines. Then, holding the layers together, cut around the shape, including the tab.

9. Fold one of the boots in half, then fold the tab inside the boot, glue it and press hard. Make the other boot in the same way.

Treasure chest

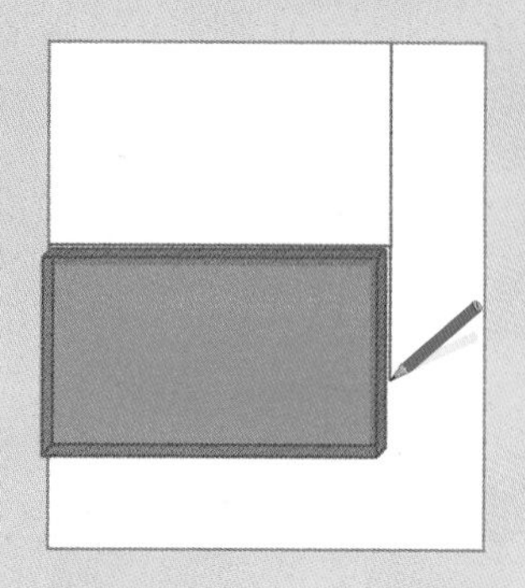

1. For the top of the chest, lay the lid of a shoe box on a large piece of thin cardboard. Then, draw around it twice, like this.

2. Cut around the shape, then cut a strip off one end. Then, cut one of the long sides off the lid of the shoe box.

3. Tape one of the short edges of the cardboard along the remaining long side of the lid, using lots of small pieces of sticky tape.

4. Fold up the edge of the cardboard that hasn't been taped. The folded part will be glued onto the box, to make the chest's hinge.

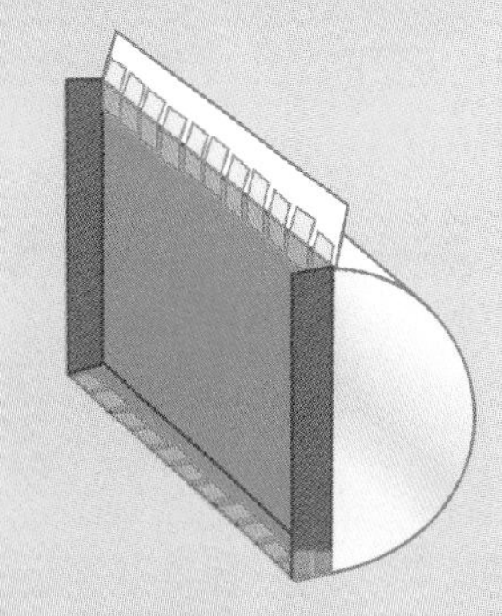

5. To make the top curve, tape the folded edge of the hinge to the lid, like this. Secure it with lots of small pieces of tape.

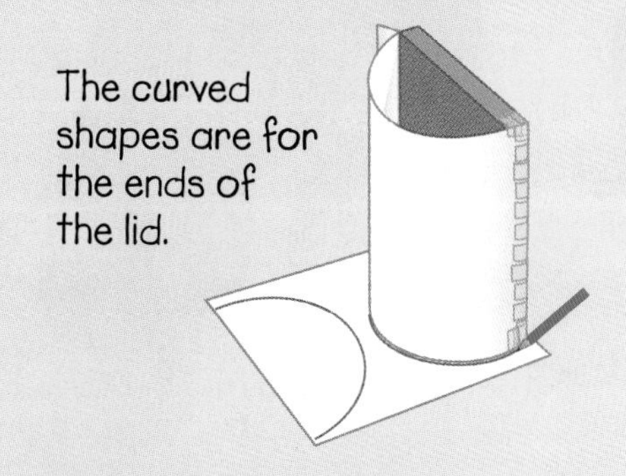

6. Place one end of the lid at the edge of a piece of cardboard. Draw around the curve, then move the lid. Draw around it again.

7. Cut out the curved shapes. Then, tape one shape onto each end of the lid, matching the edges as well as you can.

8. Put the lid on the chest. Spread white glue along the edge of the chest, then press down the hinge and tape it, to secure it.

9. When the glue is dry, gently open the lid of the chest. Then, tape all the way along the hinge, inside the chest.

Put the chest on a newspaper.

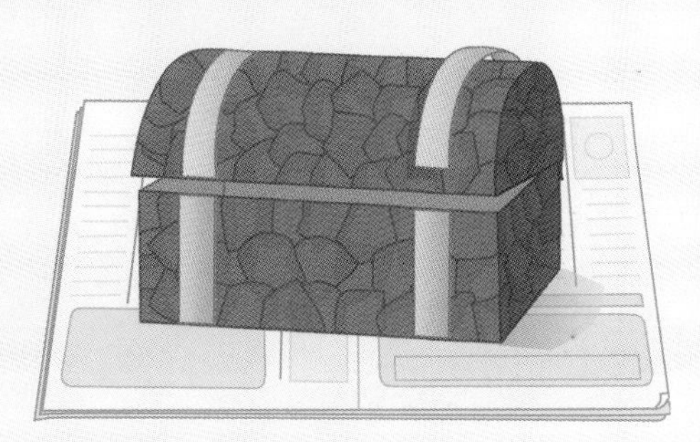

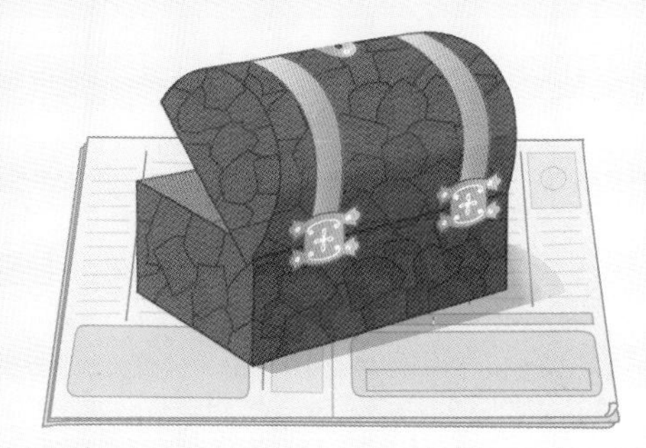

10. Rip lots of tissue paper into large pieces. Brush glue onto the chest and press on pieces of tissue paper, until it is covered.

11. For straps, cut two strips of paper, and glue them onto the front of the chest. Then, glue two longer strips onto the lid.

12. Press the lock and hinges from the sticker pages onto the front and back of the chest, or draw your own and glue them on.

Fill your treasure chest with coins (see page 6), jewels and other shiny treasure.

Shiny cutlass and hook

Cutlass

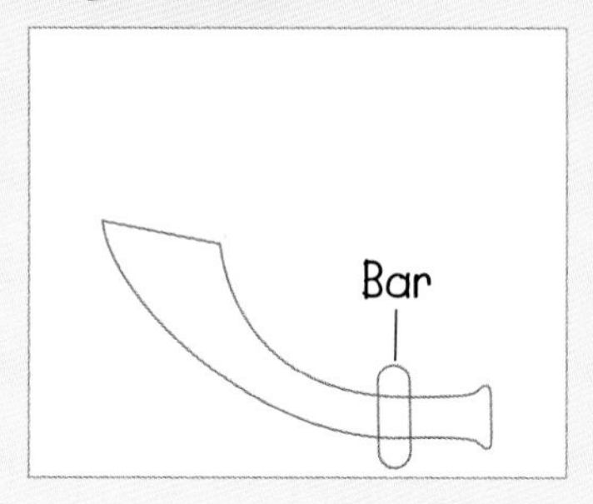

1. Draw a curved shape for the blade on a large piece of cardboard. Then, draw a handle with a bar across it, at one end of the blade.

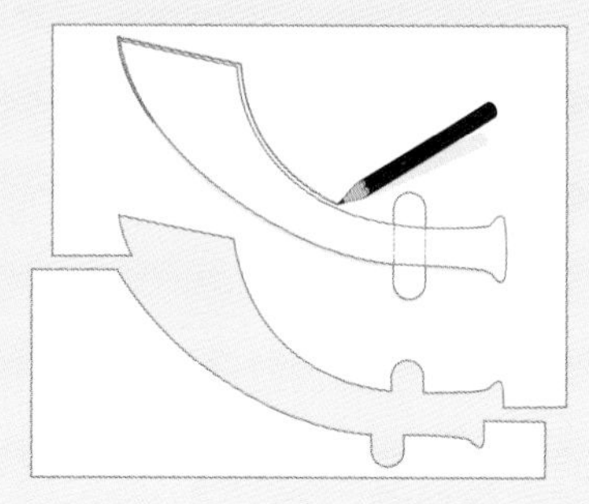

2. Cut out the cutlass, then lay it back on the cardboard. Carefully draw around the cutlass, then cut out the shape.

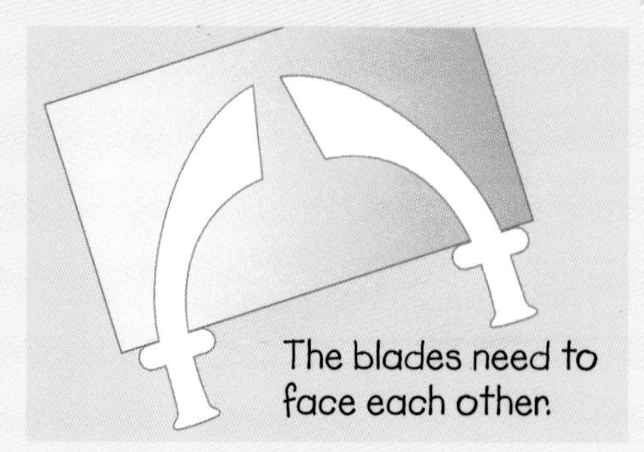

3. Spread glue on one side of each blade. Press them onto a piece of kitchen foil, with the handles sticking off the edge, like this.

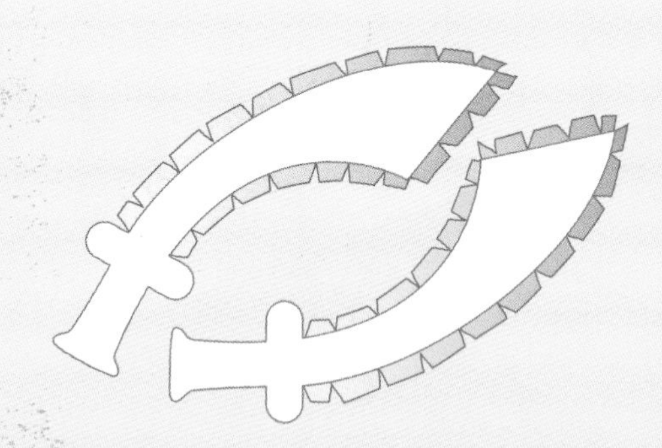

4. Cut around the blades, leaving a border. Then, make V-shaped cuts all around the border, to make the foil easier to bend.

5. Spread glue around the edge of each blade. Bend the foil over the edges and press it down. Then, glue them both together.

6. Lay the handle on some brown or gold paper. Draw around it, then turn it over and draw around it again. Then, cut out the shapes.

7. Glue the paper shapes onto the handle. Then, decorate the handle with bright or shiny paper, foil, or stickers from this book.

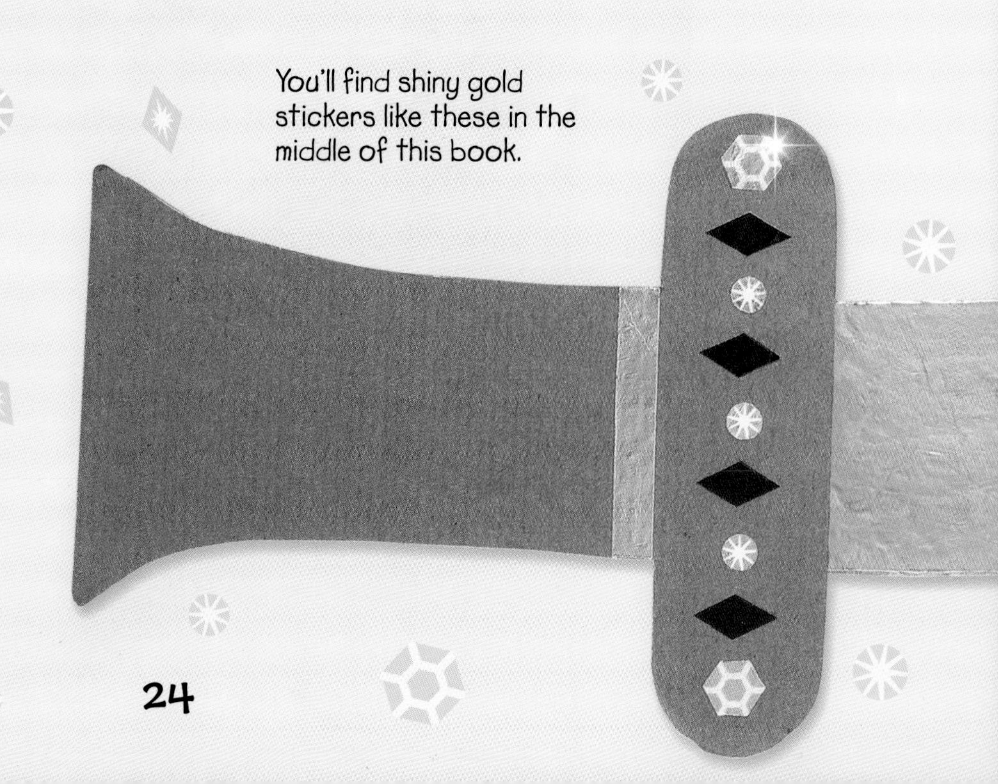

You'll find shiny gold stickers like these in the middle of this book.

Hook

1. Draw around a large mug on a piece of cardboard. Then, draw curves for the blade. Add a handle with a bar across it.

2. Cut around the outline of the hook, then lay it back on the cardboard. Draw around it again, then cut it out.

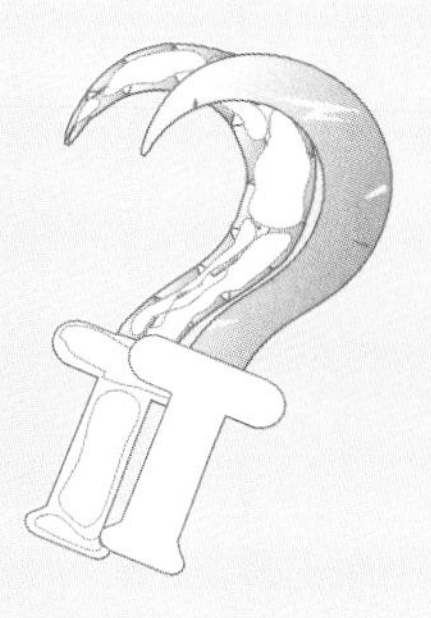

3. Following steps 3-7 opposite, cover the blades with foil, then glue the hooks together. Glue paper onto the handles, too.

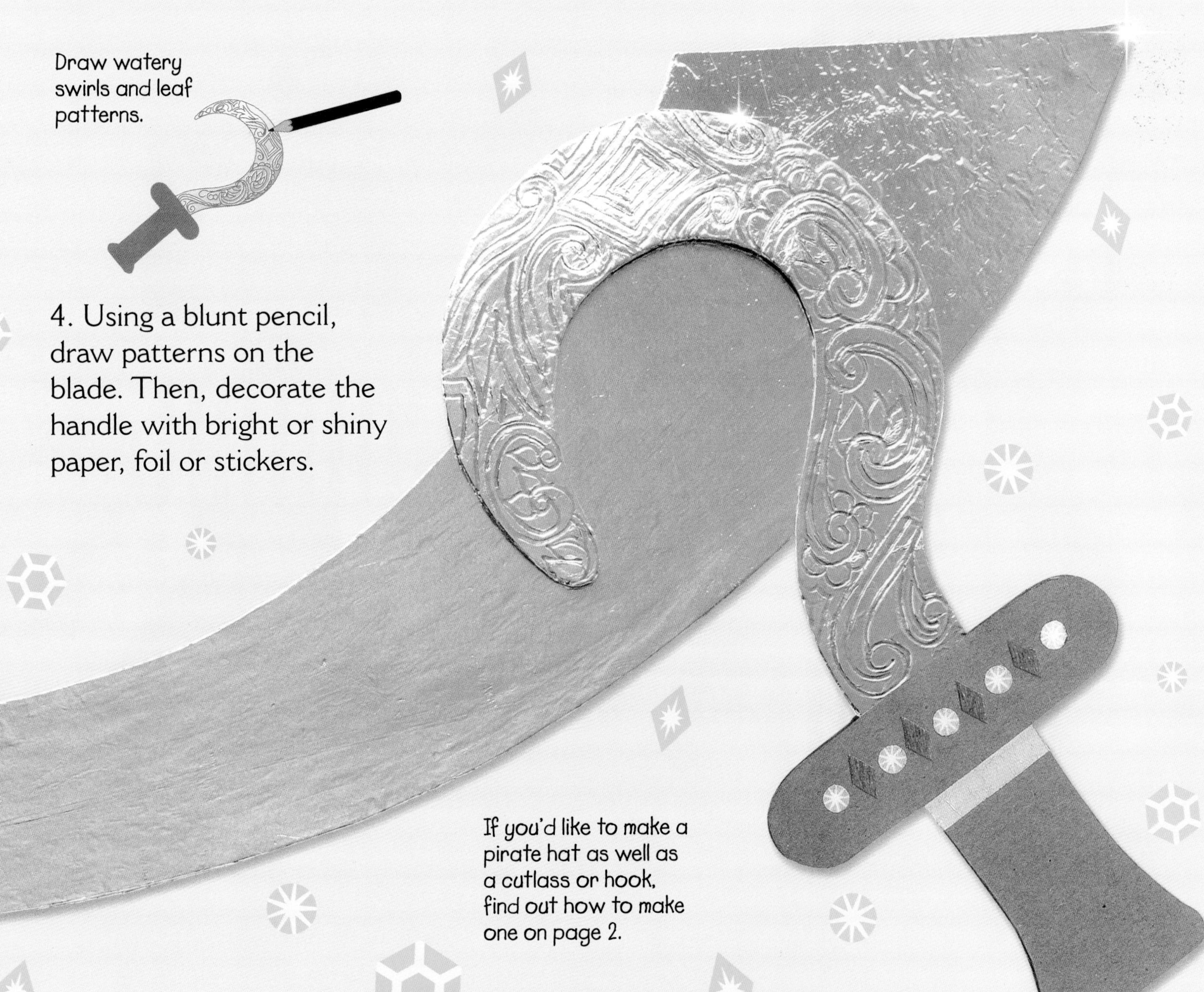

Draw watery swirls and leaf patterns.

4. Using a blunt pencil, draw patterns on the blade. Then, decorate the handle with bright or shiny paper, foil or stickers.

If you'd like to make a pirate hat as well as a cutlass or hook, find out how to make one on page 2.

Pirate crew collage

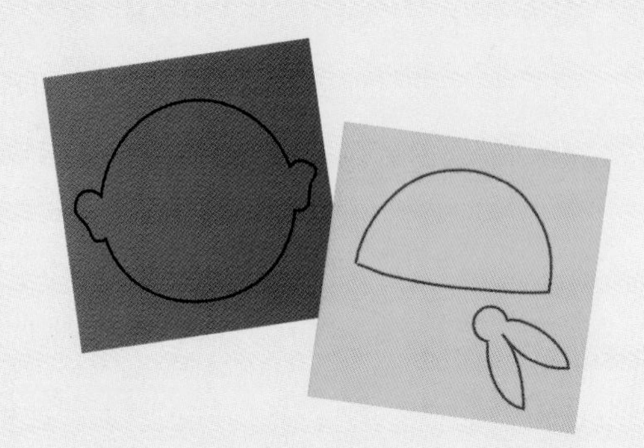

1. Using a pencil, draw a pirate's head on paper from an old magazine. Then, draw a scarf and a knot on another piece of paper.

2. Cut out the shapes, then glue the scarf and knot onto the head. Cut out some hair and glue it on. Then, draw a face.

3. Glue the head onto a big piece of paper. Cut a rectangle from striped paper for the pirate's top. Glue it on below the head.

Try making a girl pirate, with pretty clothes and jewels.

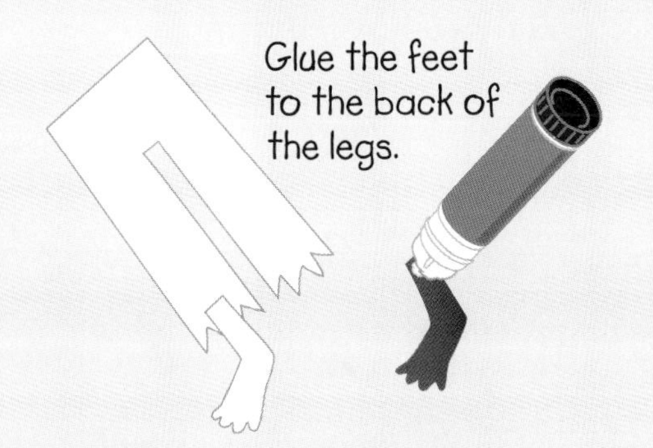

4. Cut out ragged legs and feet from magazine paper. Glue the feet onto the legs, then glue them below the pirate's body.

5. Cut out two sleeves and hands and glue them together. Then, glue the arms on either side of the pirate's top.

6. Cut a strip of paper and glue it on, for a belt. Then, cut two shapes for the waistcoat and glue them on, overlapping the arms.

Cut-out galleon card

1. Fold a long rectangle of thick paper in half, with its short ends together. Then, slide a piece of light blue paper inside the card.

2. Draw around the front of the card. Then, slide a piece of darker blue paper into the card and draw around it, too.

3. Cut out the shapes. Glue the light blue one inside the card. Then, draw a wavy line across the other shape.

To make a desert island card like this, make a tall, thin card in step 1.

4. Fold the card again. Then, cut along the wavy line and lay the waves on the card. Draw along the top edge of the waves.

5. Draw a pirate's galleon with masts, sails and flags, overlapping the wavy line. Then, go over the lines with a black felt-tip pen.

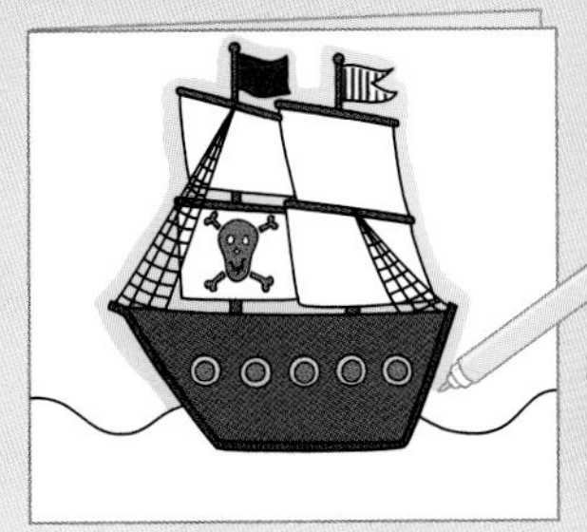

Use a pen that matches the paper inside the card.

6. Fill in the galleon with felt-tip pens. Add some sky between the sails and around the galleon, but don't fill in the waves.

Leave a border of sky around the edge of the galleon.

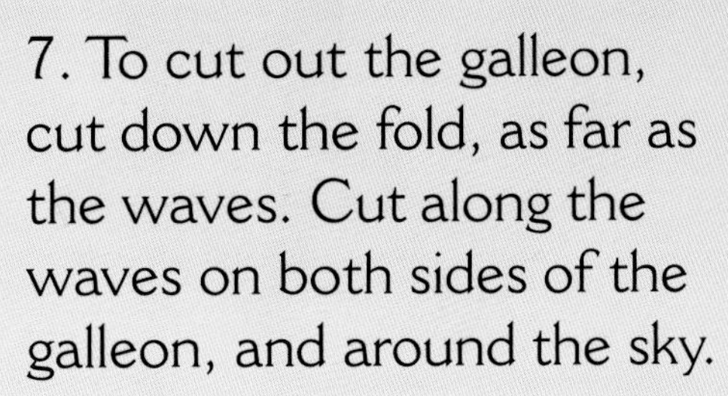

7. To cut out the galleon, cut down the fold, as far as the waves. Cut along the waves on both sides of the galleon, and around the sky.

8. Glue the waves onto the card. Then, cut shapes for little waves and glue them on. Glue paper clouds onto the sky.

You could paint
some bright flowers
on the tree.

Paint lots of green
leaves around the
parrot, too.

Painted pirate's parrot

1. Draw a shape for the parrot's head and body, on a large piece of paper. Make the shape twice as long as your hand.

2. Draw an eye and a beak. Add some feathers on the side of the parrot's head. Then, draw a branch and two feet, like this.

3. Using yellow paint, fill in the beak and the feet. Then, when the paint has dried, paint the body and the head with red paint.

4. Using long brushstrokes, paint a red tail. Let the paint dry, then add yellow feathers on top. Then, paint green feathers, too.

5. On an old plate, spread red, yellow, green and blue paint in stripes. Then, press your right hand into the paint, across all the stripes.

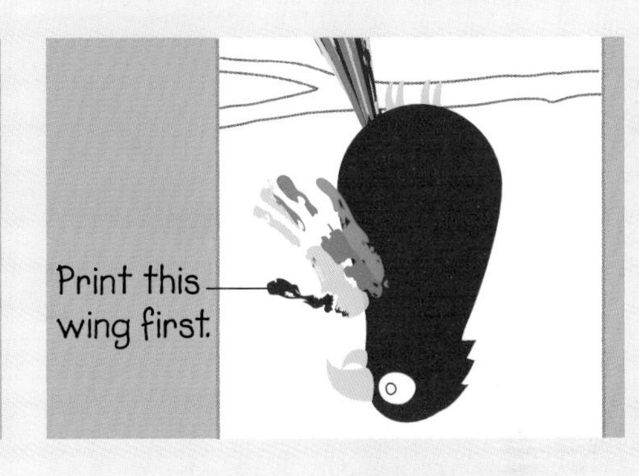

6. Turn the paper upside down. Then, using your hand, print a wing on the parrot. Make it overlap the parrot's body, like this.

7. Turn the plate around, so that the red paint is on the right-hand side. Then, print the parrot's other wing with your left hand.

8. Wash your hands, then paint a black dot on the eye. Leave the paint to dry. Then, paint the branch, using thick brown paint.

Jolly Roger paper

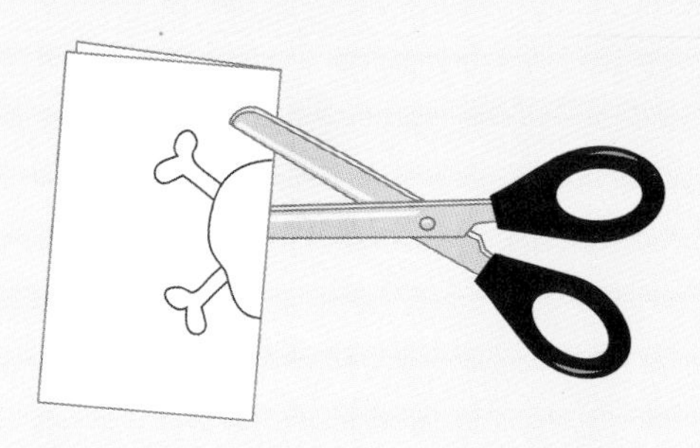

1. To make a stencil, fold a piece of thick paper in half. Draw half a skull and two bones against the fold, then cut along the lines.

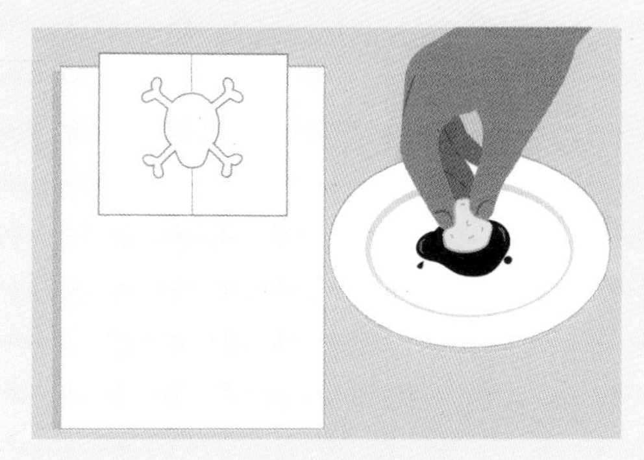

2. Open out the stencil and lay it on a flat piece of paper. Spread some paint on an old plate, then dip a sponge into the paint.

3. Dab paint all over the hole, then lift off the stencil. When the paint is dry, draw eyes, a nose and a toothy grin on the skull.

You could decorate wrapping paper, gift tags and envelopes, too.

Photographic manipulation: John Russell
First published in 2005 by Usborne Publishing Ltd., Usborne House, 83-85 Saffron Hill, London, England. www.usborne.com
Copyright © 2005 Usborne Publishing Ltd. The name Usborne and the devices are Trade Marks of Usborne Publishing Ltd. All rights reserved.
No part of this publication may be reproduced, stored in a retrieval system, or transmitted in any form or by any means, electronic, mechanical, photocopying, recording or otherwise without the prior permission of the publisher.
UE First published in America in 2005. Printed in Malaysia.